the *Lifestyle* shoppe

Robert Alan Ward

This is a work of fiction. All of the characters, names, incidents, organizations, and dialogue in this novel are either the products of the author's imagination or are used fictitiously.

WestBow Press books may be ordered through booksellers or by contacting:

WestBow Press
A Division of Thomas Nelson & Zondervan
1663 Liberty Drive
Bloomington, IN 47403
www.westbowpress.com
1 (866) 928-1240

ISBN: 978-1-9736-0546-1 (sc)
ISBN: 978-1-9736-0545-4 (hc)
ISBN: 978-1-9736-0547-8 (e)

Library of Congress Control Number: 2017916488

Print information available on the last page.

WestBow Press rev. date: 01/15/2018

"Enter by the narrow gate; for the gate is wide, and the way is broad that leads to destruction, and many are those who enter by it. For the gate is small, and the way is narrow that leads to life, and few are those who find it." Matthew 7:13-14

Based on the musical, "The Lifestyle Shoppe"

by Robert Alan Ward

Music and lyrics by Alisha Jane Keating

Lyrics to the song "We are Gods"

by Robert Alan Ward

To Richard Haskell

Who many years ago told me about
Jesus Christ, and helped
me start my journey on the narrow road that leads to life.

PROLOGUE

As I walked through the wilderness of this world, my soul grew weary of perpetual war and human cruelty. In my weariness, I found a cave where I lay down and slept.

While I slept I dreamed a dream. In my dream, I saw a young woman making her way up the main thoroughfare of the city of Commonplace. She was of medium height and build. Her hair was a simple brown, unimaginatively combed to the sides. Her shirt and jeans, along with the rest of her, seemed to blend with the commonplace surroundings.

With her she carried a shabby purse that contained the sum of her earthly possessions, an ID card and one hundred dollars from a foster agency. The money had been allotted to her earlier that day, her eighteenth birthday, her final day in "the system." For the first time in her life she was alone, though in truth, she had never belonged.

She studied the faces of those who passed by—faces that

ignored her, except as a collision to avoid. Women came in pairs or trios, chattering emptiness. Men did likewise, though with fewer words and less animation, unless they spoke of sports. She wondered what was truly going on in the lives of those collisions to be avoided.

Are they as lost, as am I? The earth revolves aimlessly around the sun. The sun rises. The sun sets. I was born and I will die—as will they. When I am gone, the earth will continue on its pointless path—and who will miss any of us? Why do I exist?

That simple four-word question had been haunting her thoughts for some time. As of yet, she had no answer. Yet still she clung to hope. She had been told of a place for people like her—people searching for a reason to exist.

Finally, she came to her destination, a non-descript building, on a non-descript street corner, in the non-descript city of Commonplace. Above the entrance hung a sign with three simple words: THE LIFESTYLE SHOPPE.

CHAPTER 1

For long minutes, the young woman stood motionless outside, apprehensive of the unknown. Finally gathering the courage, she tentatively entered the shop. As her eyes scanned the surroundings, her first impression was the size, which appeared far greater than suggested from outside. Aside from the spacious reception area, what she could see of the shop consisted of three rooms, one to her left, one in the center, and the last to her right.

The room to her left was by far the most attractive, filled with dazzling sights and sounds. The room directly in front of her appeared the most challenging, at least at first glance. To her right the third room showed no outward sign of enticement. Neither could she see as far into it as she could the other two. Yet it held somewhat an air of mystery, as if it might contain treasures not evident to the casual viewer. A solid curtain hung on the wall between the center room and the mysterious room to her right.

She peered again into the room to her left. For the first time, she noticed the word "Broadway" brilliantly displayed on a tall, curved sign that stood at the entrance of a wide, long boulevard. On either side of Broadway was an assortment of shops, all festively adorned. As if drawn by an invisible magnet, she approached the sign. The closer she came, the greater became its pull.

Yet though she found the attraction great, she had determined to know the other parts of the shop before committing to any one room. With difficulty, she backed away from the alluring enticements. Once again at the center of the shop, she turned her attention to the middle room. A ladder that reached nearly to the ceiling stood alone at its center. Around the ladder was an expansive area that somewhat resembled a fitness center, with a number of exercise machines throughout. Pictures adorned the walls of people who appeared to have accomplished something. A long table on one side of the ladder displayed sports equipment, military medals, trophies, ribbons, and certificates. On the other side of the ladder and was another table, featuring a model of the downtown section of some large city, complete with tall buildings; the newer, the taller.

What does all of this mean? she wondered.

She backed away from the center room. "Hello?" she called out. "Is anybody here? Hello?"

Through the curtain that hung to the right of the middle room emerged a short, slightly rotund, middle-aged man. He wore thick black glasses. Curly hair that seemed to explode from both sides above his ears, accented a shiny baldpate above. A white apron and a black bow-tie completed the look.

"May I help you, young lady?" he cordially inquired.

"I hope so," she replied somewhat timorously. "My name is Seeker. I'm searching for a life. I was told that I might find something here."

The shopkeeper nodded thoughtfully. "You have come to the right place. This is the Lifestyle Shoppe. People come here from all over the world to try on different lives. Would you like me to show you around?"

An involuntary smile found its way unto Seeker's face. "I would appreciate that very much. Thank you."

"All right." He pointed to the room on her left. "Let's get started over here with Broadway. This is by far the most popular room in my shop. If all you're looking for is a good time, this is the place to get it."

From just outside the room Seeker again surveyed the scene, which now teemed with people. It certainly appeared captivating, with all its bright lights, brilliant colors, and delectable looking treats, all of which vociferously vied for her attention. A sign she had not seen before, with the words "eat, drink, and be merry" flashed on and off above one of the shops.

"It does seem attractive," she remarked with considerable understatement.

"Indeed," replied the shopkeeper. "We had to make this street extra wide in order to accommodate the many people who buy here."

The shop door clanged open and a hefty, innocent faced teen who appeared to be about the same age as Seeker entered. He wore a blue baseball cap, a simple red T-shirt, and blue jeans. He afforded cursory glances at the rooms to his right and in the middle. A huge smile broke out upon his face when he saw Broadway. Immediately he entered and quickly disappeared into the crowd.

"Well," remarked the shopkeeper. "It didn't take long for young Gullible to make up his mind."

"What will become of him?" asked Seeker.

The shopkeeper shrugged. "You never know. Sometimes they turn out all right. More often, you never see them again."

Her eyes focused on a particularly interesting shelf that stood in front of the nearest shop. "Could you explain that shelf there?"

"Of course. That's Self Shelf—where all you think about is yourself."

"That doesn't sound very noble."

The shopkeeper chuckled. "Noble would have to be found elsewhere."

She peered again at the "eat, drink, and be merry" sign. Is that all there is to this place?"

"Pretty much."

"It seems like I ought to be worth more than this."

The front door again clanged open and another young man in a plain, olive drab uniform entered. "Federal Parcel Service," he announced, as if his voice were a recording.

"Good morning," said the shopkeeper. "What have you got for me today?"

The deliveryman lugged in an assortment of packages, all neatly stacked on his flattened hand-truck. "Looks like we've got all Striveway stuff for today. Let's see," he said as he stacked them at the entrance to the middle room. "We've got political issues; liberal, conservative, feminist, whatever. Here's philanthropy. Here's athletic accomplishment, ending poverty, saving the environment. Here's world peace—an exercise in futility if you want my opinion. Oh! And here's religion. Sign here, please."

The shopkeeper signed on the window provided and handed the computerized record keeper back to the deliveryman. "Thank you, young man. Have a nice day." With that he was gone.

"Excuse me," said Seeker, pointing to the middle room. "How are the people who buy in this room different from the Broadway people?"

"Well technically," he answered, "Striveway is a part of Broadway, even if it doesn't appear so at first glance. But in answer to your question, Striveway buyers are more focused. They do better quality work. They accomplish things. But by focusing on one area, they often miss the broader spectrum of life. And sometimes their definitions of success come at a heavy price."

Seeker's eyes fell again on the tall ladder. "Why is that ladder standing by itself in the middle of the room?"

"That, young lady, is one example of what I mean by a

heavy price. That is what's known as the corporate ladder. People strive to reach the top, which as you can see, has room for only one. The fight for the top often becomes savagely brutal, as the participants attempt to dislodge their rivals on the way. And as I said, those who so engage often neglect other important aspects of their lives, such as their families."

"What do you do once you get to the top—if you get there?"

"You try to stay as long as you can. But once you're there, you become everyone's target." The shopkeeper became strangely quiet. "It's a lonely place. None stay at the top forever. A few retire peacefully. Those who don't are eventually toppled—and great is their fall. Some end up in prison or otherwise ruined. Eventually, they all die."

Seeker shook her head sadly. "Then why do people strive so hard to climb that ladder?"

"It's called Striveway, my lady. Those who go this route want power. They want prestige. They want the finer things in life. And there's a certain thrill in the climb."

"Which leads to nowhere, and then they die."

For a third time the front door opened, this time revealing a large, imposing man in tan shorts and a white T-shirt that fit tightly to his chest, emphasizing his rippling physique.

"Hi there, Jock," said the shopkeeper.

"Hi," he answered. Without another word, he strode straight into Striveway.

"That was Jock Revere," said the shopkeeper. "He too knows exactly what he wants."

Seeker looked at the shopkeeper imploringly. "He may know what he wants. Gullible may know what he wants. But I don't know what I want. All I know is that I've only got one life. Is there anything more worthwhile than what I've seen so far?"

The shopkeeper gestured Seeker to the far-right side of the shop, to the modest looking room she had little noticed before. On a small table by the entrance to the room lay a large, thick book. Above the table was a simple wooden sign.

THE WAY IS NARROW THAT LEADS TO LIFE

She turned quizzically to the shopkeeper. "What does that mean?"

"To those who prefer a libertine lifestyle, Narrow Way means too many restrictions. To those who choose Striveway, it is too humbling. That is why this is the least traveled room in our shop. As you can see, the entrance is quite narrow and not particularly attractive on the outside—no fancy displays—no bright coloring. And it's by far the most difficult room in the shop. Sometimes people browse here at the front out of curiosity, or even briefly go in before heading elsewhere. But those few who enter and stay, develop a quality about them that I don't see anywhere else."

"Can you describe it to me?"

"It's a little hard to put your finger on. You'd never understand why, but they actually seem to have more fun than the Broadway people. The simplest things bring them joy. Yet they don't become addicted to them."

He pointed to the book. "They have a unified outlook on life, based upon the transcendent principles contained in that book, that brings everything into balance and perspective for them."

"That doesn't sound so difficult."

The shopkeeper chuckled. "Oh, but it is. These people are constantly going uphill, and always against the grain of popular culture. They choose virtue over vanity, discipline over indulgence, and honesty over personal gain. And I've noticed that they're often not well liked by many of the people who shop elsewhere."

"You'd think that even those who shop elsewhere would still appreciate an honest person."

"Some genuinely do. But to most others, their way of life serves as a rebuke. People don't like being rebuked."

She turned again toward the narrow door. "So, you're saying that Narrow Way costs the most?"

The shopkeeper rubbed his chin thoughtfully. "Look at it this way, my friend. It will cost you anywhere you buy. You pay the least for Broadway up front. But Broadway tends to cost you more and more down the road. You pay more for Striveway up front. There's usually a period of good times in the middle, but then the price goes up steeply toward the end. Narrow Way has to be thought of as an investment. It costs by far the most initially, but then pays increasing dividends down the road. And if you believe the people who buy here, they'll tell you that the dividends never stop."

"When you put it that way, it seems like I'd be a fool to buy anywhere else."

"Well now, that's up to you. I'm just the shopkeeper."

Seeker stared long and hard at the narrow door. "All right. How much will it cost me to buy at Narrow Way?"

The shopkeeper looked at her soberly. "Everything you've got—now, and for the rest of your life, for the author of the book has stated, 'If anyone wishes to come after Me, let him deny himself, and take up his cross daily, and follow Me'."

Seeker shook her head sadly. "I was afraid you might answer something like that." She backed away from Narrow Way to again view the three rooms from a distance, temporarily paralyzed by indecision.

"I'll tell you what," she finally declared. "May I go as an observer into each of the rooms before making my final decision?" She pointed to Broadway. "I'd like to start there."

"Window shop?" asked the shopkeeper. "Certainly. I'm content to be patient. Sooner or later, everyone buys from the Lifestyle Shoppe. But in order to enter any of the rooms, I require first a one-hundred-dollar retainer fee." He looked at her earnestly. "Contrary to popular opinion, nothing in life is free."

Hesitantly, she opened her purse and handed him all the money she had.

CHAPTER 2

Having known disappointment before in her life, Seeker entered Broadway more with trepidation than anticipation. She found the broad boulevard crowded with shoppers, bustling in and out of the many shops that lined each side. As she laboriously made her way up the street, voices from the various shops called out to her.

"Come aside here! Find riches the fast and easy way!"

"Come! Eat of my delicacies and find happiness!"

"The end of your search is here! Take our mind-expanding potions and explore the inner recesses of your intellect!"

"Fame this way in three easy steps!"

In truth, she had already heard many of their pitches before and knew them to be dubious. She continued on, if for no other reason than to find something new.

Near the far end of the city, the crowd began to thin out.

There, quite by chance she spotted Gullible, whose size, blue baseball cap, and red T-shirt made him stand out. He was surrounded by a group of boys who looked older than himself and one still older adult in flashy attire, who held a tan leather satchel. His face sported a neatly trimmed goatee beneath a thick scalp of immaculately groomed raven hair. Curious of Gullible's chosen path, she approached to within earshot of the group, feigning interest in a window display to mask her presence.

"Come with us," the older adult was saying. "Let us lie in wait for blood. We shall find all kinds of precious wealth. Throw in your lot with us. We shall all have one purse."

Out of the corner of her eye, Seeker studied the faces of the other boys in the group, all of which appeared hardened beyond their years. When the comparatively innocent faced Gullible consented, several of the older boys slapped him on the back. With that they disappeared through a doorway into a seedy looking building. Seeker shook her head in dismay, fearing that Gullible's decision would not end well. Yet she remembered the words of the shopkeeper. "Sometimes they end up all right." Maybe there was still hope for him.

Turning her gaze onward, she spotted a misty cloud hovering on or above the road in the distance. *Now that looks like something new.* As she made her way toward the cloud, the boulevard began to narrow. At length, the paved street ended and she found herself on a dusty dirt road. For her, the quiet of the countryside was a welcome contrast to the din of the city. The cloud, which she now saw to be at road level, was swirling a slow, counter-clockwise rotation.

Upon entering the misty fog, the temperature noticeably cooled. For several minutes Seeker continued, wondering what might be on the other side. The enveloping fog became so thick that only with difficulty could she see her hand, which she held in front of her for fear of running into something. Her pace slowed to a crawl.

Finally, the fog began to abate. The forms of trees began to take shape before her eyes. She emerged into a large park under dreary, overcast skies. The park was laid out in a perfect square, with city surrounding it on all sides. At its exact center stood a large fountain, bounded by benches, some occupied and some vacant. A massive oak tree overshadowed the fountain area.

Instinctively, Seeker made for the oak tree. Once at the tree, with the fountain's cascading waters yielding pleasant ambiance, she turned full circle to take in the scene. A few evergreen conifers towered above a larger number of deciduous trees, including maples, elms, and oaks, all colorfully arrayed in full fall foliage. A man in a business suit sat alone at a nearby table reading a book while eating his lunch. Others of less savory appearance lingered about. A mother holding a dog on a lease with one hand, pushed a stroller containing a small child on a cement walkway with the other. In the distance, a group of young boys were engaged in a spirited soccer game. The misty portal through which she had entered the park was nowhere to be seen.

Upon completing the circle, her eyes focused for the first time upon a young teenage girl approaching in her direction. She was of medium height with auburn hair. She wore a light gray jacket and a pair of fitted blue jeans, with thread-bare marks in various places. In her right hand, she clutched a small travel bag. As she drew closer, Seeker noted her flawless, olive toned complexion and her perfectly formed facial features. *Beauty queen material,* thought Seeker, *except for that lost, forlorn look in her eyes.*

"Hello," she called out. "My name is Runaway. What's yours?"

"Seeker," she replied. "What are you running away from?"

Her walk took on a more confident swagger as she

closed the remaining distance between them. "A prison, masquerading as a home," she brashly replied, somewhat out of breath. "Want to go looking for the good times together?"

How does this girl know she can trust me? wondered Seeker. "What do you mean by the good times?"

"I mean good times—fun, excitement, adventure—anything but the dull, boring life I had at home with my dull, boring parents."

As the two conversed under the great oak tree, another woman, older and with a pronounced stoop slowly approached the fountain. She was clad in a faded green overcoat that sported several moth-eaten holes. Her brownish gray hair sat like a messy mop under a dull blue scarf on top of her head. She sat down on one of the benches, facing away from the fountain. From her tattered purse emerged a bag from which she began tossing bread crumbs to a gathering cluster of pigeons.

"Here you go pigies. Sorry I'm late today."

Runaway gave Seeker a cocky, streetwise look. "Watch me charm granny out of some cash."

She sauntered over to the older woman. "Excuse me, ma'am. I'm stranded in this town. It's a long, sad story. Could I borrow a few dollars?"

"I'm sorry," the woman replied, a tinge of sadness in her voice. "I don't have any money."

Visibly deflated, Runaway turned back to Seeker. "Are you hungry?" the older woman called.

She put her hand on her stomach and stood frozen in her tracks for a moment. Slowly she turned back to face the older woman. "Yes."

"There's half a donut in this bag you can have. Sorry if it's a little stale."

She approached just close enough to reach for the donut. "Thanks." She began to nibble on it, as if it might be her last meal for a long time.

"My name is Baglady. I come here every day to feed the pigeons. They're so used to it now; they're always here waiting for me."

"Do you live around here?"

"Most of the time."

Runaway cautiously took a seat at the far end of the bench. "Do you know a place around here where someone can stay without money?"

Baglady pointed behind her, toward the south side of the park. "There's a rescue mission three blocks from here. They'll put you up for a night."

A period of awkward silence followed. Runaway fidgeted, not knowing what to say or do next. Finally, the older woman broke the silence. "You're pretty young to be out on your own."

"I can take care of myself," Runaway indignantly replied.

Baglady continued to feed the pigeons, as if she hadn't heard the angry retort. More silence followed. As Seeker observed, it became increasingly obvious that Runaway's haughty outward demeanor was beginning to crumble.

"I had to get away," the young girl finally blurted out.

Baglady turned her face to listen.

"My parents don't understand me. All they want is to boss me around. They have to meet my boyfriends. They have to check my school work. I have to be home by a certain time. Why can't they trust me? They treat me like I'm a little child!"

The older woman slowly contemplated Runaway's words before responding. "It sounds to me like they love you."

"Then why do they have to treat me like that?"

"Maybe they know something you don't?"

"Like what?"

Baglady tossed another handful of bread crumbs to the pigeons. "It's a pretty tough world out here."

Runaway nudged slightly closer to the older woman. "You could show me how to make it."

"I thought you said you could take care of yourself."

"Well, I can. I just need a little coaching."

A tone of sternness entered her voice. "You want a little coaching? Go home."

Tears began to form in the corners of Runaway's eyes. "I can't go home. It would be humiliating. And then my parents would mess up my life even more!"

Baglady threw the last of her breadcrumbs to the pigeons. "Sorry, pigies. That's all for today." She turned her attention fully to Runaway, a sad, somber expression on her face.

"Have you ever been the parent of a teenager?"

"No."

"But your parents have been teenagers?"

"I suppose."

"So your parents know what it's like to be where you are, but you don't know anything about what it's like to be where they are."

"Teenagers are different now!"

"You're right," exclaimed Baglady with a hint of sarcasm. "They don't need homes to live in—or food—or schooling—or any kind of rules. They don't need any of that anymore."

"Well, I'm not going to boss my kids around like they were doing to me!"

"Of course not. You'll just let them play on the freeways until they get themselves killed."

"No, I won't!"

Another period of silence ensued until Runaway finally asked the awful question she knew she had to ask. "Do you really think I should go home?"

Baglady looked her young friend in the eye. "Long ago, I did something like what you are doing. It turned out to be the worst decision of my life. Now I wish I had a home to go to—and people who loved me."

"I thought you said you lived around here."

She laughed a sad laugh. "Oh, I do—in the bushes—in abandoned buildings. It gets cold. Occasionally they let me stay at the rescue mission—whatever I can find."

"How do you eat?"

"There's a regular circuit of churches and soup kitchens that feed the homeless on different days. I scrounge dumpsters. I collect plastic bottles for money. I live in constant fear of being robbed—or worse. Ain't much of a life. Are you sure you want it?"

Runaway's outward façade finally dissolved into tears,

all outward pretension lost. "But how can I face my parents again after this?"

Baglady put her arm around the young girl's shoulders. "I'd rather face two parents who loved me, than a whole world I wasn't ready for. Do you have a cell phone?"

Through her tears Runaway shook her head. "My parents took it from me."

The older woman struggled to her feet and extended her hand to Runaway. "Come on. I'll take you to the rescue mission. They'll let you call home from there."

Runaway looked up at Baglady. Hesitantly, she accepted the hand.

Seeker stood back and watched almost enviously, as the unlikely duo made their way toward the south side of the park and the rescue mission beyond. *If only I had a place to call home—and people who loved me.*

They had not gone twenty steps before suddenly there emerged from behind another tree the same raven-haired man Seeker had seen before with Gullible. "Where are you headed?" he asked, his eyes focused on Runaway.

"To the rescue mission," she answered.

The man laughed disdainfully. "The rescue mission?"

He pointed derisively at Baglady. "That's a place for bag hags like her—not quality people like yourself."

"Who are you?"

"Dregs Donotrooth at your service. Dregs is the name. Adventure is the game."

Runaway's face abruptly lit up. "Where have you been all my life?"

"Honey—I know this man…"

"Buzz off, grandma," the young girl rudely interposed. She turned again to Dregs. "When do we get started?"

"Why wait?" he replied. There was a leering, lecherous look in his eyes. He produced a neatly wrapped treat from his leather satchel. "Here—have a little Corinthian candy to sort of loosen things up."

As Dregs handed Runaway the piece of candy, Baglady, realizing that her counsel was no longer needed, silently padded away. Eagerly, Runaway popped the candy into her mouth. Almost immediately, her taste buds revolted at the foul taste.

"It's an acquired taste," said Dregs. "Here—have another."

Hesitantly, Runaway took the second piece, unwilling to

admit that she hated both the taste and the dizzying effects of the candy.

"What's the matter? Can't you take it?" he mocked.

"I can handle it," answered Runaway in a brash attempt at bravado. She quickly downed the second piece, which almost as quickly sent her reeling. With great difficulty, she staggered back to the park bench and sat down.

"Like I said—it's an acquired taste. Come on. Let's go."

He pulled her to her feet and pointed to his car at the north end of the park, a little more than a football field distant. For the first minute, she walked a crazy zigzag path in the general direction of the car. Had Seeker not felt a deep foreboding within, she might have laughed at Runaway's pathetic effort. Dregs, possessing no such compunction, deliriously derided her until he grew inpatient. He took hold of her left arm and guided her straight for his car. Once there, he opened a rear door and shoved her into the back seat. With that he got behind the wheel and sped off. Silently, instinctively, Seeker spoke a prayer for her friend, whom she knew to be in danger.

An acute sense of drowsiness suddenly overcame Seeker. She sought again the ostensible security of the great oak tree by the fountain. There beneath its sheltering canopy she curled up and fell asleep.

CHAPTER 3

Seeker awakened to a penetrating early morning frost. Shivering, she sat up and placed her arms between her thighs for warmth. The green grass of the park was nowhere evident under a covering of new fallen snow. The trees, which had exhibited an impressive array of fall colors, were now barren. A smattering of light, airy snowflakes gently descended from above.

She stood to her feet, wondering where she could go to get warm, her attire being ill suited for winter conditions. She looked hopefully for the portal through which she had entered the park, but saw nothing. Scanning her surroundings, she noticed for the first time an attractive, single story building that stood across the street from the south end of the park. Smoke pouring from the chimney told her that there was warmth to be had inside. On the roof of the building was a sign with lettering too small to read from her distance. Cold, combined with curiosity getting the best of her, she began to make her way for the building. The snow crunched under her feet as she walked, gradually numbing them. As she approached, the words on the sign came into focus.

DOCTOR OLGA FALLACIOUS, THE
ANSWER TO ALL YOUR TROUBLES

I wonder if she can cure my troubles? From across the street, Seeker stopped momentarily to survey the building. Though it appeared attractive on the outside, she wondered why the shades were pulled down at every window, including the panes on the front door. She crossed the street and headed up the walkway.

The warmth of the reception room was an immediate and welcome relief from the bitter cold of outside. Seeker immediately made for the fireplace and stood facing it, savoring the pleasant sense of thawing out. For the first time, she noticed the fragrant scent of peach blossoms emanating from several large candles.

She turned around to thaw the other side and for the first time took in the room, which emanated a cozy friendliness. The knotty pine paneled walls were adorned with several

Norman Rockwell paintings. The furnishings had a rustic, comfortable, inviting appearance.

An attractive, smartly dressed woman appeared from behind the expansive, waist level opening between the reception room and the front office. "Good morning, young lady. We're so glad you have come. What can I do for you?"

"I saw the sign on the roof. Can you really solve all my problems?"

The woman gave a slight chuckle. "I am not the doctor. But I can arrange a free consultation for you with Doctor Fallacious in just a few minutes if you'd like."

A series of mental calculations whirred their way through Seeker's mind. *The offer seems too good to be true. But what if it is true? What if I walk out of here, always wondering what I missed? Besides, the consultation is free and it's cold outside. What do I have to lose?*

"I would like that very much."

"Well then," said the receptionist. "Follow me to the consultation room."

She pointed to a door. Reluctantly, Seeker parted from the warmth of the fire and met the receptionist on the other side. Down a long corridor they went. Along the walls were pictures of smiling people, all with glowing testimonies of the miracles Doctor Fallacious had wrought in their lives. At the end of the hall the receptionist opened a door on her left. She handed Seeker a clipboard with an attached pen.

"Please answer the questions on the sheet. It will help Doctor Fallacious work her miracle for you. She'll be with you in a few minutes."

With that the receptionist left, leaving Seeker alone in the room. Before filling out the questionnaire, she took off her shoes and socks to rub some circulation into her feet. She looked about the room. More framed testimonies hung on the walls. Several magazines, all woman centered, were strewn haphazardly on two different counters. An examination table stood prominently in the middle of the room.

Before she could observe further, the door suddenly swung open and a slovenly dressed man entered. A too short T-shirt and too low shorts failed to cover a too bulging belly. He wore a funny looking beige hat that looked like it might have been found lying in the middle of a busy intersection. With him he carried a large jug. On the side of the jug was a prominent skull and crossbones symbol. The word "poison" was inscribed below it.

"How's it goin', babe?" he bellowed as he closed the door behind him.

"My name is Seeker," she answered, somewhat taken aback by his effrontery.

"Yeah? Well I'm Scott Free. I do what I want." He took a healthy gulp from his jug and wiped his mouth with the back of his left hand.

"Why do you drink poison?"

"Because it tastes good." He seated himself on the examination table and gave Seeker a disconcerting look.

The door opened again to reveal a slightly overweight, short woman, who appeared to be in her thirties. She wore a white lab coat and no makeup. Her brown hair was cut decidedly short. Around her neck was wrapped a stethoscope. Over her left pocket was a nameplate that read Doctor Olga Fallacious. She seemed unaware of Seeker's presence.

"Good morning, Mr. Free."

"Mornin', Doc."

"And what miracle can I work for you today?"

"I ain't been feelin' well. I got this gnawing pain all through me. Don't have any idea why." He took another swallow from his jug.

"Well," observed the doctor, "if pain is your problem, then you need a pain killer." She retrieved a small container from a medicine cabinet. "Here you go. These are fifty dollars. You can pay me directly."

"Fifty bucks?!"

"Hey. Do you want to feel better or not?"

"Fifty bucks," he again muttered under his breath. He opened his wallet and carelessly tossed a fifty-dollar bill on the table, which the doctor quickly stuffed in her right lab coat pocket. He grabbed the bottle, took out two capsules, and washed them down with more poison.

"One at a time," cautioned the doctor. "And there is another issue. How long have you been drinking like that?"

"Whoa now doc," answered the man indignantly. "I ain't givin' up my drinkin'. Scott Free always does what he wants."

Doctor Fallacious threw up her arms in protest. "Oh, I wouldn't dream of suggesting abstinence. But you really ought to consider the use of sterilized containers."

"I suppose you want another fifty bucks for a batch of those."

The doctor shook her head. "There's a government agency here in town that distributes them for free. It's all part of our government's 'safe poison drinking' program."

She dug a business card from a drawer under the counter

and handed it to Free. "Here's the address and hours of operation."

He scrutinized the card. "Free, huh? Just like me. I'll have to check it out." He stood up to leave, again lifting the jug to his mouth.

"Ah ah!" admonished the doctor. "Only from sterilized containers."

"Right."

With that Doc Fallacious departed the room. Free immediately took another gulp and gave Seeker a second unnerving stare. Then just as suddenly, he turned and departed, loudly slamming the door behind him.

For several minutes Seeker sat, pondering the strangeness of the experience. *Safe poison drinking? Didn't the doctor even see me?*

When it appeared that the doctor would not return, she put her shoes and socks back on, and made her way to the reception room. The well-dressed receptionist was nowhere to be seen. The fire had died down to a smolder, devoid of the heat it formerly produced. The door to the outside lay open, apparently left so by a departing "too much effort to close it" Scott Free. An inner voice told Seeker that, cold notwithstanding, it was time for her to leave too. Out of simple decency, she closed the door as she left.

Somewhat bewildered, she wandered back to the park and headed straight for the fountain, more out of familiarity than anything else. By now it had stopped snowing and the sun had begun to peek from behind the clouds, affording at least some relief from the bitter cold of the earlier part of the day. She brushed a two-inch layer of snow off the same bench where Baglady and Runaway had been and sat down.

"How's it going, hon?" called an unpleasantly familiar voice from behind.

Immediately, Dregs Donotrooth, who again appeared to have materialized from nowhere, came around to the front of the bench. "How about it, hon? Are you ready now for some fun, excitement, and adventure?"

"I am not your hon," she answered indignantly. "And where's Runaway?"

"Who?" He pondered for a moment, searching his mind. "Oh, that girl. She's old news. Time to move on."

"Old news? I thought she was a human being. Where is she?"

"I have no idea."

"What about Gullible?"

Dregs gave her a surprised look. "How do you know about Gullible?"

"I have eyes," she enigmatically replied.

"Yeah, well he got caught." He shook his head dismissively. "I always teach my boys that it's a sin to get caught. He didn't listen very well."

He sat down on the bench, uncomfortably close to Seeker, laying his leather satchel on the other side. "It looks like it's you and me now."

A feeling of abhorrence pulsed through her. "I have no wish to be old news. So it's just you—and it's just me."

She rose from the bench and strode rapidly away, direction being less important than distance. "Why did you come here if you weren't looking for a good time?" he called after her. She gave no reply, but only increased her pace, hoping that he would not follow.

CHAPTER 4

For hours Seeker aimlessly wandered the city streets, wondering where she should go and what to do next. The sun, which had been providing some warmth, fast began to lose its effect as it arced toward the western horizon. Her stomach increasingly protested its neglect. She wished she still had the one hundred dollars she had been given on her final day as a ward of the state. Unfortunately, it was in the hands of a shopkeeper, whom she doubted she would ever see again.

Out of sheer exhaustion and in an attempt to assuage her hunger, she finally sat down on the sidewalk and put her head down, using the wall of a building across the street from the park as a backrest. *Maybe I can dream my way back to the shop.*

For some time, she shivered in a half sleep. Near nightfall, the tantalizing aroma of hot food awakened her senses. Numbly, she struggled to her feet to ascertain the source of the offerings. Across the street large group of people were assembling in the park, not far from the fountain.

"Gather around everyone," came a voice over a public-address system. "Food for the stomach. Food for the soul."

At least the first part sounded good to Seeker. She crossed the street and got in line behind a group of shabbily dressed individuals whom she guessed were homeless, as indeed was she. While she waited, a group of singers, mostly women, stood on a portable platform, singing strange songs that somehow brought comfort to her soul. After two songs, they departed the stage and a young man wearing an ill-fitting, second hand suit climbed the steps to replace them. He stood behind a microphone and began to speak incomprehensible words about some ancient man and eternal life. Looking around, she saw that a few were listening. The remainder were engaged in conversations of their own with others in the long line.

When her turn came, a middle-aged woman on the other side of the serving tables took a Styrofoam cup from the top of a high stack and ladled it to the top with hot chicken noodle soup. Seeker looked hungrily at the more substantial food readily evident.

"What about the other food?" she asked the middle-aged woman.

"We serve only soup first," she answered sweetly as she handed the cup to Seeker. "After the message is finished, we serve the main course. That's how we make sure the people stay for the message."

Very well, thought Seeker, glad to at least get something hot into her while she awaited the main event. She sat down on a nearby bench, sipping her soup while she surveyed the crowd, hoping to catch sight of either Runaway or Baglady. Neither was anywhere to be seen.

The message continued long after her soup was gone, but at last the man finished with a prayer of thanksgiving for the food and Seeker again stood in line. When finally it came her turn, she fairly drooled over the chicken casserole, corn, salad, bread, fruit, and cookies spread out of the tables. The middle-aged woman gave Seeker a telling wink and heaped her plate a little fuller with casserole than the others. After sitting down again, she devoured the entire fair in less than five minutes.

Her stomach fully satisfied, the next task was to see if she could find a warm, safe place to get a shower and sleep the night. She approached the middle-aged woman with the sweet voice, whom she thought would be sympathetic to her plight.

"Where can someone stay the night around here without money?"

The woman sadly shook her head. "The Rescue Mission would be the place, but it's always full by this time. You have to get there no later than 3 p.m. on a given day."

She looked Seeker up and down. "Do you not you have anything warmer to wear?"

Now it was Seeker's turn to shake her head.

"Come with me."

She followed the middle-aged woman around to the rear of the portable stage, where three long tables were set up, all with various types and sizes of clothing and shoes. The woman picked out a faded blue trench coat that looked like it might fit Seeker.

"Here—try this on."

While Seeker donned the trench coat, the middle-aged woman found a ski cap and placed it gently over her nearly frost-bitten ears. She selected some heavier walking boots that looked to be Seeker's size and two pairs of clean socks. "These will help too." Finally, she handed the younger woman a thick woolen blanket. "And this will help too."

Seeker stared at the woman incredulously. "Why are you doing this? No one has ever been kind to me like this before."

"We are people who walk the narrow way that leads to life," she answered. "This is what we do. That is what the message was about. I wish I could do more."

Embarrassed, Seeker simply nodded her head. The only message she truly understood had come from the middle-aged woman. She also wondered why she was meeting Narrow Way people in Broadway. "Thank you very much, ma'am. What is your name?"

"Grace. And I believe that your name is Seeker."

Startled, Seeker stared at her in wonderment. "How did you know?"

"I can always tell the seekers from those who just want to eat. Seek, and you shall find."

With that Grace parted to tend again to the cleanup. Seeker sat on the same bench she had been before to put on a fresh pair of clean socks and her new boots, which she found to fit perfectly.

She was just finishing the task when a familiar figure emerged from the far side of the great oak tree. She wondered why she hadn't seen her before. The young woman tossed her empty plate and utensils into a trash can and made her way in the direction of Doctor Fallacious' office. Her steps were heavy and trancelike, as if she were heading to her execution. After watching for a while, Seeker felt in inner urge to follow. It was obvious that the girl had some kind of deep problem. She wondered if Doctor Fallacious would be able to fix it, as the sign promised. Inwardly, she had her doubts.

No fire burned in the fireplace when Seeker entered, a few seconds behind the other girl. The receptionist barely acknowledged the first girl and pointed to the entry door. She went through the door and down the long hallway to the consultation room. Seeker followed about ten paces behind. Once in the room she sat down opposite the young woman. No words transpired between them as they silently waited. *For what?*

Finally, Doctor Fallacious entered. She looked tired and eager to end her work day.

"Good evening, Runaway," she said in a businesslike tone. "The results are back. Your test is positive."

"Oh no!" sighed Runaway in anguish. "What do I do now?"

"You do the only sensible thing. Do you have any money?"

Her head dropped in despair. "No."

The doctor appeared disappointed, but quickly recovered

her professional demeanor. "Well, I can get the government to pay for it. It's just slower that way."

"No one ever told me that this would happen," she moaned.

"You didn't take the proper precautions. But it's still okay. I can take care of your problem for you."

"But is it right?" asked Runaway, looking up with forlorn eyes. For the first time Seeker noticed tears. "I mean, is it right to take care of my problem?"

"Of course, it's right. It's your right to choose."

With that the doctor began to sway in rhythmic fashion, as if another entity were taking over her body. From her lips came a bewitching tune that seemed to cast a spell upon the frightened girl.

Young child I've seen that look of fear before
The one that says I don't know where to go
You found love in another's arms that night
And now your heart lies broken on the floor

You have come alone to this place
And alone you must leave
For this world is already filled
With the results of too much passion

Come with me, I have an answer

It's not a matter of right or wrong

How can a decision that affects you alone

Be made by anyone but you?

Why don't you just carry on and live your life

Or will you really just live on to carry?

Come with me, I have an answer…

Just think, by this time tomorrow

You can be a free woman

Nothing holding you back

Independence, the greatest liberty

No one telling you, 'you were wrong'

No one even knowing what you've done

Others who judge

What do they know about loving choices?

It's your choice, come with me

It's a good choice, come with me

It's the smart choice, come with me

It's the only choice, come with me

You have no other choice, come with me

The doctor placed her right hand in the small Runaway's

back and led her from the consultation room, closing the door behind them. Down the hall Seeker listened through the door as Runaway's crying turned to sobs. Another door closed. The sobs turned to shrieks.

• • • • • • • • • • ● • • • • • • • • • •

And then in my dream I saw Seeker approach the fountain in the blackness of the night. A bone chilling cold had set in that would only intensify with the hours. Silhouetted against the city lights on the north side, Seeker discerned a solitary figure seated at the same bench by the fountain, crying softly, her back turned. Coming from behind, Seeker gently placed her hands on Runaway's shoulders in a hopeless, but sincere effort to inject comfort into the distraught young woman.

"I have blood on my hands," wept Runaway, as the frost from her breath dissipated into the air before her. "And no matter what I do for the rest of my life, nothing will ever undo what I have done."

Seeker came around the bench and sat down next to her friend. She wrapped her blanket around the two of them, thinking to at least provide some warmth, which she herself also needed.

"Come with me, Runaway," she offered. "Let's leave this place."

The young girl turned her face away. "You go, Seeker. It's too late for me. All I want is to die."

"There's a better life somewhere else. Come with me and let's find it together."

Runaway shook her head. "It's too late for me. Go—before it's too late for you." From the depths of her agony came a pitiful cry.

I was searching for a life so beautiful
All I found was life full of death and despair
I can't go back to the life I used to know
I can't go forward towards a life absent of hope

And I am left alone with my fears
And I am drowning in my tears
And you can say there's a life worth living
But my soul has died with my hope

My bleeding heart won't last,
It can't take the pain
My strength is fading fast
Please just leave me here to die

I can't go back to the life I used to know
I can't go forward towards a life absent of hope

And I am left alone with my fears
And I am drowning in my tears
And you can say there's a life worth living
But my soul has died with my hope

With that, Runaway seemingly dissolved into the air like a breath. Seeker found herself alone on the bench—weeping uncontrollably.

CHAPTER 5

A dense darkness descended upon my dream, where I saw only despair for what seemed an endless period of time. As light gradually returned, I saw that Seeker had somehow returned to the Lifestyle Shoppe. In her hands, she held a small hand towel, which she was using to dry her tears.

"So, young lady," the shopkeeper asked, "What did you discover about Broadway?"

She handed the towel back to him and composed herself. "I discovered that the negative consequences of Broadway lived lives far outweigh the pleasure."

The shopkeeper nodded his head. "The loss of innocence—either deep sorrow or the loss of conscience—or both. The loss of time and potential—and ultimately of hope."

"Yes. I saw all that when I was there. But I still have hope—and I might have gained something from my experience. If I do find a 'better,' it might seem better still from the contrast."

"Perhaps. Where would you go next?"

Seeker turned her eyes toward Striveway. "How about this place?"

"Striveway? Very well. Just walk into the room." He handed the towel back to Seeker. "You may still need this. Good luck to you."

No sooner did Seeker enter the spacious room, when an open doorway materialized on its far side. Aromatic scents and pleasant sounds poured from the opening, enticing Seeker past the corporate ladder and through the doorway. Once through, the room behind her immediately vanished. She found herself in the midst of a picturesque, fragrant garden. Sunlight filtered through the leaves and branches, and the pale pink blossoms of a cherry tree above her. She gazed in wonder at the lush fuchsias, birds of paradise, morning glories, passion vines, and numerous other exotic flowers, all in full bloom.

A firm dirt path led her to a small clearing. There a carved, finely finished oaken bench sat before a pond that teemed with small to medium sized fish in a myriad array of colors. On the surface of the pond floated several patches of lily pads, whose blooms exploded in rich hues of pink and gold. A small stream flowing from above fed into the pond, which overflowed on the other side, keeping the equilibrium. The low hum of bees and the bright chirping of birds in an endless display of colors combined with the stream to yield pleasant ambiance.

She seated herself on the bench and basked in the idyllic scene, all the while taking in deep breaths of sweet air. For some minutes, she remained until she heard the sound of approaching footsteps and of happy, carefree young voices. Quickly she arose and hid herself behind a thickly laden passion vine, not wanting to disturb the moment, but also wishing to witness another of the joys of Striveway.

A young couple emerged into the clearing, holding hands, lost in a state of dreamy blissfulness. Seeker's eyes went first to the girl, whose flowing shimmery chestnut hair framed a tanned, pure complexion. The sparkle in her eyes set her in marked contrast to Runaway. She wore a colorful silken top, with black leather slacks, both of which accentuated her statuesque, perfectly proportioned figure. A pair of high ankle orange colored boots, combined with the rest of her outfit, provided her an air of pleasant sophistication.

The young man, with his thick head of bronzed hair and

athletic face seemed the perfect match. He had on a casual blue blazer over tan Levi style jeans. His feet sported a pair of blue loafers. On his left wrist was a shiny gold watch that screamed for attention. He had the look of a man who was going somewhere—and who would be equally at home if that somewhere were an athletic field, the corporate world, or the halls of academia.

The two sat down and drank in the sights before them. "It is so beautiful and peaceful here," remarked the young lady."

The young man nodded pleasant agreement. "Beauty all around us, but especially next to me." At his words, the young woman blushed and snuggled closer to him. He took hold of her left hand.

"You know, Misty, I am doing very well at Energy Unlimited. I'm making a good salary. My boss told me that there's no limit to my potential. He says I have great communication skills and wants to use me for public relations speeches."

He turned his eyes fully toward her. "But all of that will be meaningless, unless I can share my life with someone special." He peered deeply into her eyes. "Someone like you."

A look of rapture burst upon her face. "Harrison? Are you asking me what I think you're asking me?"

The young man rose from the bench and went to one knee before the young lady. He clasped her left hand between both of his. "Misty Greentree, will you marry me?"

"Oh, Harrison," she answered. "I would totally love to be your wife!"

He leaped to his feet exultantly and began to dance in celebration, as if he had just scored a touchdown. "Yes! My name is Harrison Foxtrot, and I am the happiest man in the whole world." He turned to Misty. "I'll make it good for us. We'll have a big beautiful home, nice cars..."

"fine clothes, fancy furs, jewelry…"

"Speaking of jewelry."

He reached into a pocket in his blazer and retrieved a small, bright red box. Holding it before her eyes, he opened it. There in the box sat a ring, with a large iridescent diamond at its center. He lifted the ring from the box and slipped it on to her left, ring finger. She gazed adoringly at her prize, waving it about in wondrous ecstasy.

"We'll have a beautiful life together."

"We'll live happily ever after! If you are the happiest man in the world, then I am the world's happiest woman!"

She stood to her feet and threw her arms around her husband to be. For a full minute, they held their embrace before they began to kiss passionately.

Finally finished, they floated arm in arm, deeper into the garden. For the first time, she noticed Seeker, who made like she had just arrived at the place. As Misty passed by, she dreamily showed off her ring before the young lovers disappeared from view behind a stand of bluish-purple morning glories.

That was so sweet, thought Seeker. *Happily ever after. Maybe this is the place for me.*

She sat again on the bench before the pond, wondering if perhaps a man like Harrison Foxtrot might suddenly materialize and seat himself beside her. She held out her left hand, envisioning a similar ring on her finger.

The wondrous contemplation soon began to lose its luster when Prince Charming failed to appear. Seeker rose from the bench. *Maybe I'll have to go looking.* It seemed natural to follow the path taken by Harrison and Misty.

But after a time, she came to a fork. For several minutes she stood motionless, trying to discern some evidence as to which way they might have gone. The hardened dirt provided no footprints. With no other clues available, she simply selected the left fork, hoping she had chosen right. Soon she came to a dead end, where a wall of tall, thick shrubbery blocked the path and all vision beyond.

Concluding that she had guessed wrong, she was about to retrace her steps when the thunderous cheers of a great throng penetrated the shrubbery. Suddenly, a baseball landed on the path before her and rolled out of sight under a clump of pink and purple blooming hydrangeas. At once she determined to fight her way through the barrier to witness what sounded to be a wild celebration on the other side. She chose what appeared to be the easiest access point and committed her body to the task. Surprisingly, once she entered, the shrubbery gave way with minimal effort and no scratches.

When she emerged on the other side, she found herself standing near a television camera on the grassy playing field of an enormous baseball park. Before the camera, holding a microphone stood a gorgeous blond female television announcer. Next to her was a man in a dirt-smudged baseball uniform. Instantly, she recognized him.

"Well, Jock," intoned the television announcer. "That was quite a dramatic shot with two outs in the bottom of the ninth. Victory snatched from the jaws of defeat. You sure sent the fans home happy. You seem to have a flair for the dramatic."

"Well thank you, Giselle," he answered. "I always like to please the home folks—make them feel like they got their money's worth."

"Indeed, they did. What pitch were you looking for in that situation?"

"Anything I could drive out of the ballpark. He threw me a slider that didn't slide, and I drove it."

"So now you're three games out of first place. What will it take to catch the Bombers?"

"Just go out and win again tomorrow. One day at a time. Hopefully, I can contribute."

"Well thanks for your time, Jock. We'll see you out here tomorrow."

Indeed, this is the place for me, thought Seeker—*successful happy people everywhere. Who wouldn't want such things?*

CHAPTER 6

For a time, Seeker stood in place, wondering what to do next. She turned full circle, as she had done at the park in Broadway. Near the end of her 360-degree revolution her eyes fell on one of the many advertisements that covered the entire stadium, except for the playing field.

THE CHURCH OF LIMITLESS DREAMS

WHERE SELF-DISCOVERY IS OUR
MOST IMPORTANT PRODUCT

COME MEET PASTOR MENDACITY,
OUR GUIDING LIGHT

SEEKER FRIENDLY SERVICES

SUNDAYS, 10 TO 11AM

She turned another revolution, thinking perhaps to discover another portal through which she might visit the church. When none presented themselves, she walked up into the stands to ask directions from fans still milling about, reveling in their team's magical win.

From her pew near the back of the auditorium Seeker gazed in awe at the magnificent interior of the Church of Limitless Dreams. High above her loomed a ceiling of cedar, with a massive crossbeam that spanned the entire length of the church. Plush red carpet adorned the aisles and stage. The floor under the pews consisted of dark, richly treated wood. The elegant wooden pews were topped with cushiony gold padding. Stained glass windows, five to each side, with breath-taking scenes of nature, lined the walls to her left and her right. A glorious pipe organ was set at the left of the stage as she faced it, balanced by a deeply polished, ebony grand piano on the right. At the piano sat a handsome young man in a designer suit, playing quiet, soothing melodies.

As she scanned the crowd, her eyes fell upon Harrison Foxtrot and Misty Greentree, who sat before her and to the right. Two rows behind them sat Gullible by himself. *How did he get here?* she wondered.

At precisely 10 a.m. an impeccably dressed woman somewhere in her thirties entered from a door on the left side of the stage. She gracefully made her way to a microphone halfway between the door and the rich cherry-wood pulpit. Cued by her hand signal, the pianist began a melodic lead-in. In a whisper she began her song, which gradually built in power throughout.

We are gods, we are gods
Creatures of chance,
Evolved from the cosmos,
Destined to live and to live again in many forms

To the ever-present force we yield
All self-absorbed in oneness
All minds melded in unity,
All person lost in union
We salute you, oh great power
Oh, great something from somewhere
Lead us on to higher conscience
Lead us on to future lives

Upon finishing, the soloist silently exited through the same door from which she came. The man behind the piano descended the five steps to floor level and seated himself in a first-row pew. A woman wearing an elegant maroon pants suit, with a golden vestment lined in scarlet, rose from the same row and climbed the steps to the pulpit. For a moment, she organized her notes before looking out over the congregation.

"Good morning, enlightened ones. For those of you visiting today, I am Pastor Desiree Mendacity, your guiding light. My meditation this morning is entitled, 'Our Hidden Divinity Within'."

Her words flowed in mesmerizing, modulated tones. "All of us, be we gay or straight, transgender or lesbian, bisexual or asexual, possess a hidden divinity within. Neither is it relevant what faith one follows, or if one professes no faith at all. All of earth's peoples are one. All of us are evolved to our present state of consciousness, purely as the result of the natural forces that hum within and around us. God is all things. We are all gods. The Church of Limitless Dreams exists solely for the purpose of helping each of you discover your divinity—your particular evolutionary niche within the vast cosmos—the role you are to play within the giant machine of which we are all parts.

"Some of you seated here this morning exist, at least in this life, to make money. To you I say, 'make all you can.' It is your divine right. It is both duty and destiny for you to become rich and famous. Only remember that one-third of your income belongs to the church that brought you to self-discovery. Those who withhold will know bad karma. What goes around comes around."

"Some of you here exist to go deeper into your spirituality—to locate the spirit sources within you, in order to evolve into still higher states of consciousness—to discover new realities."

"But most of you here this morning, are what I call 'worker bees.' You are making your way from past lives of relative obscurity, on your way to future lives of ever ascending status—until you too can own worlds. To you I say, 'Bring all you can. Give all you can. Feel all you can.'"

"And then there are the ascended masters such as myself—we who have successfully navigated through past lives to our present elevated status. It is we who are charged with bringing the ignorant masses around us to awareness, through the relentless redefinition words, and of the rights and wrongs the unenlightened once took for granted—helping to usher in the New World Order."

As Seeker sat listening, she wondered if she might be one of whom Pastor Mendacity referred to as unenlightened. She had certainly never heard such a message before. It was not at all like the message given by the man in the funny suit she had only half heard at the park in Broadway. She wondered if the people at this church would ever lower themselves, like Grace and others at the park, to feed the homeless.

Upon the conclusion of the service, promptly at eleven, Seeker got up and walked out, feeling smaller and emptier than before she had entered. For several minutes she lingered to observe the many conversations between groups of people, wondering if anyone had noticed her. From somewhere she overheard that Harrison Foxtrot would be speaking the next day at the nearby conference hall.

She was about to leave when someone tapped her on the shoulder from behind. "Hello. I hope you don't mind my intrusion. It's just that I keep seeing you in various places. What is your name?"

"My name is Seeker. And I know that your name is Gullible. I keep seeing you too. I was wondering how you got here."

The young man looked downward and shook his head. "It's a long story—one of which I am not very proud. Someone told me that I needed to find a church. So here I am this morning. What about you?"

"All I seek is a life worth living. So far I haven't found it—at least not for me."

"Well Seeker, I hope you find what you're looking for. And please, if you do, would you tell me about it?"

With that he turned and walked away. As Seeker watched him depart, she wondered if she would ever see him again.

He is a troubled young man, whom I wish I could help. But what have I to offer? I am a troubled young woman.

• • • • • • • • • • ● • • • • • • • • • •

When next I saw Seeker, she was seated in the back row of the large conference hall, filled to its capacity with a highly energized crowd of perhaps two thousand. Behind the podium on the stage stood Harrison Foxtrot. He looked the epitome of success, the crowd hanging upon his every word.

"And so, the challenge before us, ladies and gentlemen, is threefold. We simply must locate and develop new petroleum resources, preferably here at home. We must simultaneously labor to further develop other energy sources, such as nuclear, solar, water, and wind. Finally, we must make more efficient use of energy in general. Rest assured, Energy Unlimited is at the forefront in all three areas—helping to keep our nation vibrant and competitive in the global economy. Thank you for listening."

The audience erupted in thunderous applause. Harrison emerged from behind the podium and quickly found himself inundated with mostly young female admirers, who charged on to the stage. Many held up their cell phone cameras, eager to appear with him in selfies.

After an indeterminable amount of time, the crowed gradually thinned out until one solitary figure lingered on the stage and only Seeker remained in the audience. "That was quite a speech you just gave, Mr. Foxtrot." From the tone of Doctor Olga Fallacious' words, it was evident that her statement was not intended as a compliment. "But if Energy Unlimited is supposed to help our country so much, why are you outsourcing so many jobs to other countries? What about the poor right here?"

Harrison stared at her and sighed. "I care about our country's job situation. But our government has made it too expensive for us to do much hiring here. Corporate taxes are too high. They keep increasing the minimum wage.

They force myriad regulations on us and expensive health insurance, covering dubious maladies. All of that adds to the cost of doing business and raises consumer prices to a level that retards sales. It just makes better business sense to outsource our jobs to other countries, where we can get the same job done more economically and thereby maintain our competitive edge."

What made perfect sense out of the mouth of Harrison Foxtrot somehow became scrambled on its way to the ears of Doctor Fallacious. Her enraged response set off a back and forth that steadily increased in volume and intensity.

"Health insurance is the sacred right of every American—not just the exclusive privilege of the wealthy!"

"Universal health coverage just makes everyone equally unhealthy, and bankrupt!"

"How can you say that? All you do is raise taxes on the miserly rich!"

"The people you call rich are the ones who make this economy go. They provide the jobs!"

"Which they outsource to sweatshops in Lower Lollapatrainia…"

"Which makes Lower Lollaspatrainians less likely to come here illegally!"

"You are so self-righteous and mean-spirited!"

"And you are so incredibly mindless!"

As Seeker remained in her seat, witnessing the spectacle, one observation firmly set itself in her mind. *Both are shouting. Neither is listening.*

The toe to toe continued until finally it stopped, more from exhaustion than resolution. Fallacious turned to leave, but not before firing her parting shot from the far side of the stage.

"I still think you're totally insensitive and mean-spirited."

"Yeah?" retorted Harrison. "I didn't know you knew how to think."

• • • • • • • • • • ● • • • • • • • • • •

The auditorium faded from view and a new scene came gradually into focus. With the sun showing early evening, Seeker found herself standing before a stately two-story mansion, freshly painted in white, that reminded her of a southern plantation home. The front of the edifice sported eight large, rounded marble columns, four to either side of the tall, wide front door. Large, well-kept rose gardens flanked a cement stairway on both sides of the entrance. Security cameras pointed in every direction, keeping silent vigil over the property. A long, newly resurfaced asphalt driveway wove its way from an iron gate that stood at some distance. Black, spiked top, iron grates enclosed the entire property, which appeared to be laid out in a square. Verdant, manicured grass, dotted with majestic, well-spaced shade trees created a peaceful serenity.

Curiosity again getting the better of her, Seeker made her way around to the rear of the mansion. Directly behind was a large barbecue area. Further out was a lavish swimming pool. A waterfall plunged into the pool from a large, artificial rock mound on its far side. Behind the waterfall was a romantic grotto with room enough for two. To the right, a high corkscrew slide promised thrills for whoever might wish to enter the pool in a whoosh. To the left of the pool was an elaborate, lighted tennis court. Behind the pool and tennis court, at the far end of the property was a large horse corral and a pristine, freshly painted barn.

Seeker marveled at the opulence until her eyes came all the way to the right, where for the first time a familiar figure came into view. Embarrassed, she set about to leave immediately until she saw that Misty Greentree had not noticed her. Cautiously she edged closer.

"Hummmm, hummmm," the young woman buzzed

as her arms waved and her body swayed to some unheard rhythm.

The dreamlike trance continued even after Seeker heard a car door slam at the front of the house. A minute later Harrison Foxtrot emerged from the sliding door, into the barbecue area. For a time, he too watched incredulously as Misty continued her gyrations, oblivious of Seeker's presence or of her husband's return.

Finally, he took hold of her and physically interrupted the concentrate. "I thought I told you to stop this nonsense. What's gotten into you lately?"

Misty's dreamy trance abruptly ended, she gave him an indignant look and pointed to her wristwatch. "You said you'd be home by three. What time is it?"

"Just a little after seven," he somewhat sheepishly answered. "I'm sorry. I had to stay late today. There was so much work to do."

"Yeah? Well I'm sorry about your cold dinner. Your tofu and eggplant parmesan bowl is in the refrigerator."

Harrison's face fell. "Whatever happened to that meat loaf dish you used to make?"

"Who gave you the right to be an animal cannibal?" she angrily snapped. With that she stormed into the house.

Only then did Harrison notice Seeker. "I don't understand her. I give her this big beautiful home to live in. I give her a nice car and fancy furs. You'd think she'd be grateful, but no. Last week, she tossed all of her furs into a supermarket dumpster. And now she won't even fix my dinner."

"Actually, she did fix your dinner. You just didn't get home when you said you would."

Harrison shook his head sadly. "What's there to come home to? She won't cook what I like anymore. She won't..." he stopped abruptly and took a new tack. "She has no idea of the pressure I'm under at work—or of the creditors I have to stay ahead of."

Seeker nodded her head sympathetically. "I hope things work out for the two of you."

"Yeah, I do too. I'm going inside to try to smooth things over."

"Good luck."

As he headed into the house, Seeker couldn't help but notice the contrast between the erect, confident bearing of Harrison Foxtrot before, and the slumped shoulders he now exhibited. More and more she was beginning to wonder if Striveway was all that it first appeared.

CHAPTER 7

Seeker gazed incredulously at the headline on the computer screen at the local library.

BASEBALL STAR FOUND DEAD

She continued reading. "Jock Revere, star outfielder for the Commonplace Celebrities, was found dead in his hotel room on Friday morning from an apparently self-inflicted gunshot wound to the head. He had recently been suspended from baseball for the use performance enhancing drugs, which dealt a crippling blow to the Celebrities' chances of catching the Bombers. Friends said that he was also despondent over the recent breakup of his fêted marriage to supermodel Candi Caine, due to numerous alleged affairs. A spokesperson for the Celebrities expressed shock and dismay over his sudden passing."

Why? He had fame and fortune. He had a wife most men could only dream of. He had everything. Why is it that so many, who have everything so right, end up so wrong?

She thought again about Harrison and Misty. *They were so in love when I first saw them. And now they have everything too. But when I saw them the last time, it was like they were total strangers.*

She rose from her chair and headed out of the library. But as she made her way, the atmosphere around her began to change, as if she were passing through a scene change taking place behind the curtain on a live theater stage. By the time she passed through the door to the outside, the scene change was complete.

She found herself again standing before the Foxtrot's southern style mansion. In contrast to the warm sunshine that accompanied her first visit, this time the skies were a dismal gray. A gentle mist was falling to the earth.

Other differences quickly became evident as she surveyed the grounds. The road from the front gate was pockmarked and covered in debris. The formally lush green, manicured lawn was overgrown, brown in patches, and filled with weeds. The nearest evergreen tree was not, the needles having turned a deathly brown. The rose gardens stood neglected. Paint was peeling from the front of the home. A putrid stench filled the air.

She circled around to the back and saw immediately the source of the stench. The water in the formally pristine pool had turned slime green, with algae growing on the surface. The waterfall stood silent. The tennis court was strewn with debris, with the center net lying on the ground, unfastened on one side.

From inside the home, Seeker heard the incessant, piercing cries of a baby, which grated on her nerves like a dentist drilling on her teeth. And then she saw Misty, going through her gyrations in the same place, oblivious to the wails of what had to be her child.

"Hummmm, hummmm…"

Her personal appearance was as run down as the property. Her formerly flawless female form had metamorphosed from hourglass to oval. Her once shimmery chestnut hair had lost its sheen and suffered from neglect. Harrison was nowhere to be seen.

Overcome by the screams of the baby, Seeker took it upon herself to attempt communication with Misty. "Hello? Hello Misty? Misty? Earth to Misty? Come in, please."

After considerable effort, Misty somewhat awakened from her comatose state. "Who calls? Why am I disturbed?"

"Because you have a baby crying for attention. What are you doing?"

"I never wonder what I'm doing," she enigmatically replied. "The whole point is to not think about what you're doing—and just go with the flow."

"You can't just go with the flow. What about your baby?"

Misty pointed in the direction of the cries. "That was a mistake. I have more important things to do now than care for parasitical drains upon the environment. I must save the earth from exploitation by the materialists, who don't understand the rhythms of nature."

"The rhythms of nature?"

"The interdependency of all living things with one another in conjunction with the inanimate. The spirit forces within and without. The..."

"What about your baby and your husband?"

For a time, Misty stared blankly, as if she was unable to make a connection. Gradually, a hint of recognition came to her face.

"He is lost in corporate cupidity. He knows nothing about

the circle of life." She returned to her gyrations. "You take and give back—take and give back—take and give..."

"When did all this start up?"

"When I realized that I was a fur trader in my previous life. And now I must do my penance as the wife of a capitalist. Maybe, if I vibe in close enough this time, I shall be able to return in my next life as a whale."

"You sound like you think that would be a promotion. I'm trying to figure out what I should be as a human."

"Look within," she declared, as the scene began to fade from my dream. "The answers are within. Go with the flow. Go with the flow. Go with the flow. Go with the flow."

• • • • • • • • • • • ● • • • • • • • • • • •

When light returned, I saw Seeker standing in the same place. Only this time Misty was nowhere to be seen. Harrison was seated in the barbecue area, staring vacantly at the moss green pool. From his mouth dangled a cigarette. His right hand held a half-filled glass of something. A bottle that appeared to be hard liquor lay upright on the table beside him, functioning as a paperweight for a thick pile of papers beneath.

"Well, have things gotten smoothed over with Misty?" she asked him.

"More like crushed flat," he responded dejectedly. He lifted the bottle and handed her the top sheet from the pile.

"Irreconcilable differences," read Seeker. "I'm sorry."

"She claims I'm too materialistic. Then how come she demands the house, the cars, the boat, the jewelry, the horses, all the money, and the child?" He shook his head. "She only wants the child, because it's an extra twenty thousand in monthly support."

Harrison stood to his somewhat wobbly feet, a look of drunken resolution on his face. "Well, if it's a fight she wants, it's a fight she'll get."

Seeker looked at him sympathetically. "I hope it works out for you."

"Yeah. Well, I guess I need to find me a lawyer."

With that he staggered roundabout in the general direction of his house until he finally disappeared behind the tinted sliding door. Again, Seeker thought of the contrast between the Harrison she had first encountered and the Harrison she had just seen.

Here I am in Striveway, searching for a life and finding nothing but death. And no one I meet seems to know why.

CHAPTER 8

My dream shifted back to the Lifestyle Shoppe, where I saw Seeker again using the towel she had been given to dry more tears.

"Well, young lady," said the shopkeeper. "It looks like you've had another rough time."

"Everything started off so well—and then it all came apart. I'm beginning to wonder if I'll ever find a life worth living."

"If you embrace despair, you'll feel better—temporarily. But I think you want more out of life than that." He looked at her thoughtfully. "You still haven't tried Narrow Way."

"I don't know. The price is so high."

"Indeed, it is."

"I don't know if I could stay with it. I might try and then fail."

"Indeed, you might. But all success is achieved at the risk

of failure. I've seen people who appeared much weaker than yourself go that way and make it."

"There's nothing satisfactory for me in Broadway or Striveway. I guess I don't have any other options."

The shopkeeper nodded his head. "Unless you want a repeat of the heartache you've already seen, you really don't. So, you're going for it?"

Seeker gave the door another hard look as she approached it. "I will go only as an observer for now. I have to see how others do it first."

"Very well. Good luck to you. Just walk through the door and into the room."

She looked anxiously at the shopkeeper. "What will happen?"

"It's different for everyone."

Seeker stood trembling before the doorway, summoning the courage to enter. More from default than anything else, she gingerly passed through the door. Once inside, her eyes darted about nervously—ready to beat a hasty retreat at the first sign of trouble. In her mind, she expected to hear organ music and find herself among church people on a Sunday morning, at a very different service than she had experienced in Striveway. Instead, she encountered nothing but blackness.

When she turned around, groping for the door through which she had entered, it too had vanished—swallowed in the blackness. For the time being, there appeared to be no way back, and no way forward. Panic set in.

But when she again faced forward, she saw a distant light at the end of a long, narrow passageway. As she groped toward the light, she instinctively held out her hands to both sides and found the wall. The passageway was indeed narrow. The more she advanced, the more the light increased, encouraging her to quicken her pace.

She began to hear voices. Yet the voices were not of joyful singing, or of preaching, or of conversation set on spiritual subjects as she expected. When finally she emerged into a large room, she knew immediately that she was not in a church.

To her left lounged Scott Free in an easy chair, jug in hand, his bellicose voice unmistakable. "She told me I had to stop drinkin' my poison or I'd die."

"She's a dangerous threat to society," agreed Dregs Donotrooth, who was pacing about the room in agitated fashion. "We've got to find a way to silence her before she undermines everything our culture stands for."

"I'll say she has to be silenced!" came the livid voice of

Doctor Olga Fallacious. "Yesterday, she deprived two of my clients of their right to choose!"

"She said that my religion was false and that I should return to married slavery!" added Misty Greentree.

"Hey now," protested Harrison Foxtrot, who stood on the opposite side of the room. "It wasn't that bad."

Misty glared at her former husband. "You're right about that, Harrison. It was far worse!"

"She told me that my lifestyle would send me to hell," summed up Dregs. "Pure hate speech! One way or another, we've got to stop her." He looked around at the angry assemblage. "Any ideas?"

"What about digging up some dirty little secret from her past?" wondered Misty.

Dregs shook his head regretfully. "She freely admits to her past. It only makes her words all the more persuasive."

"What about corrupting her?" suggested Doctor Fallacious. "We could put some kind of temptation in her path that she can't possibly resist. Then when she falls, we'll blast it in the headlines."

Dregs tapped the fingers of his left hand on his leather satchel thoughtfully, before again shaking his head. "She is surrounded by a strong network of like-minded friends. We'd have trouble penetrating that wall."

Harrison, still smarting from Misty's stinging words, now seized upon an opportunity to redeem himself, if ever so slightly. "We could make it subtle. Get her to compromise bit by bit over time. Then one day, she'll suddenly realize that she isn't any different from the rest of us."

Dregs put his hand to his chin thoughtfully. "We're getting closer. But we need something that works faster."

"What if she had an accident?" offered Free. He picked up a piece of hard rock candy from the dish next to him. Holding it high, he dropped it to the floor. "What if she fell off a cliff?"

"Too risky," answered Dregs. "We need something just as effective, but not so messy. Come on, people. There has to be something."

Doctor Fallacious suddenly snapped her fingers in inspiration. "What if we got laws passed against bigoted, puritanical, judgmental, guilt-inducing, homophobic, hate speech? We could start off with fines and increase the severity from there."

"At the current time, we don't have quite enough public opinion on our side," answered Dregs. "But we're working on it. It takes time to completely condition the idiot masses away from their old narrow-minded dogmas about right and wrong."

"Beer and circuses—that's all the people want. That's all I want," said Free.

Dregs abruptly dropped his satchel to the floor and gestured with his hands for all other deliberation to stop. "Beer and circuses. We can speed up the process of negative public opinion by giving the people beer and circuses. But how?" He pondered for a moment.

"The media! What if we were to put her on the Dregs Donotrooth Show?"

"What is the Dregs Donotrooth Show?" asked Harrison.

"I don't know. I haven't invented it yet."

He picked up his satchel and began again to pace back and forth in deep thought. "But it'll be along the lines of our nation's modern-day circus—a presidential debate. Supposing we were to entice her on to my show with nice words like 'Here's a wonderful opportunity to present your message to others.' We let her say a little bit..."

"And then zap! We rip into her from every side," finished Doctor Fallacious. "We get her twisted around and humiliated. We manipulate the crowd against her—and from that we sway public opinion to pass laws against bigots like her."

"You've got it," exalted Dregs, pumping his fist in the air. "We'll tell her it's a friendly debate. In fact, it will be a show."

"All right," exclaimed Harrison. "The Dregs Donotrooth Show it is. I'll put the financial package together to underwrite it."

"And no doubt you'll make a hefty profit from it," interjected Doctor Fallacious.

"Hey. You want to get rid of her because she's costing you money. I want to make money off getting rid of her. What's the difference?"

Doctor Fallacious angrily marched across the room for round two. "I provide an important service for women, that also helps sustain earth's delicate ecological balance, through legitimate population constraint."

"And your ocean polluting, ozone thinning, climate changing, labor exploiting, greed-driven profit obsession is destroying the planet!" added Misty.

Harrison stared at the two incredulously. "I'm actually quite fond of this planet. What planet are you two from?"

A spirited squabble ensued until Dregs finally stepped in. "All right, that's enough. Come on, people. We may not agree on a lot of things, but we can all agree that our greatest threat is this woman. Now—you've all got work to do and I have a show to think up. Let's get to it."

Everyone but Harrison filed from the room through a doorway Seeker had not noticed before. Thinking perhaps that he lingered to create distant between himself and his former wife, she used the opportunity to approach him.

"Excuse me, Mr. Foxtrot. What is it about this woman that makes her so dangerous?"

For a rare, embarrassing moment he stood flustered, at a loss for words on how to respond. "Well," he finally offered, "she's a psychological terrorist. Guilt is a very destructive emotion."

"And you don't feel guilty about what you're going to do to her?"

Again Harrison awkwardly searched for words to justify his action. "We can't have people like her going around upsetting everyone." He looked at his watch. "Excuse me. I've got things to do. Have a nice day."

With that he disappeared through the same door that seemed to materialize in front of him, as it had with the others. Seeker again found herself alone—and bewildered.

This is Narrow Way?

CHAPTER 9

For some minutes Seeker sat contemplating her next move in the same easy chair that had held Scott Free. There appeared to be no way back to the Lifestyle Shoppe. In truth, there appeared to be no way out of the room at all, except through the door that Harrison and the others had used—the same door that now wasn't there.

Narrow Way has brought me here. Why, I don't know. But it seems that I ought to follow up on what I've seen so far. As the shopkeeper said, we never know specifically what life will bring us, no matter which path we choose. It's different for everyone.

She rose up and approached the wall where the door had been, half expecting a door to appear—half expecting nothing to happen. She came within a few inches of the wall and confirmed the latter of the expectations. *Now what?*

She remembered a saying she had heard somewhere before. "Knock, and it shall be opened to you." She raised her right hand and knocked on the wall. Immediately, a doorway materialized before her.

Passing through, she suddenly she found herself inside the same auditorium where Harrison Foxtrot had given his Energy Unlimited speech. But now the stage was arrayed in dazzling colors. Four plush royal blue chairs sat aligned on the left side of the stage from the audience's viewpoint. Below and in front of the stage was a studio orchestra of some twenty-five musicians. Though the seats were filled with people of all ages, the capacity crowd had a youthful feel to it.

The conductor raised his baton and the orchestra members snapped to attention. For one eerie moment, the entire hall was silent as the audience sat in rapt anticipation of the show that was about to begin. The kettle drum player began a long roll.

"Ladies, gentlemen, and those of alternative orientation," came an unseen voice with an edgy, 'show biz' attitude. "It's time for the Dregs Donotrooth Show—where we uncover a new fraud every day. Dregs is the name. Exposure is the game!"

The conductor's baton came down and the orchestra lit into a splashy tune. A troupe of female dancers in dazzling outfits, six from each side, rushed in from the wings, dancing a lively, somewhat scintillating choreography. The audience responded with whistles and hoots. The dancers continued their routine for some two minutes before exiting at the end of the music. Another drum roll ensued.

"And now," came the voice. "Let's welcome our host—the personification of progress—the patron of pluralism—the epitome of excess...Mr. Dregs Donotrooth!"

The orchestra erupted into another lively refrain. Dregs burst upon the stage sporting a bright Hawaiian shirt, with a lei around his neck, khaki pants, well-oiled tan boots, and his trademark leather satchel. He strutted about the stage as if he owed both it and the people before him. After milking the audience for all it was worth, he motioned for the conductor to stop the music.

"Who claims to possess the truth, whatever that is," he intoned in an authoritative voice. "Who professes to be good, and spreads a message of hate in the name of love? The answer? A so called born-again Christian—our fraud of the day! To properly expose this counterfeit, we have assembled a non-biased panel of four distinguished guests. First, let me introduce to you a man who's done it all—and he's proud of it. Please welcome Mr. Scott Free!"

With the orchestra playing its third jazzy melody, Scott

Free emerged, holding his jug in his right hand. Between chugs, he acknowledged the wildly cheering audience. At the perfect moment, almost as if his moves had been rehearsed, he shook hands with Dregs Donotrooth and sat down on the farthest of the four chairs supplied for the panelists.

"Next," spoke Dregs, "a person who has been a tireless champion for women's rights everywhere. Please give it up for Doctor Olga Fallacious!"

Doctor Fallacious entered smiling, wearing a bright red pantsuit. Loud applause greeted her entrance, more from the atmosphere of the moment than from the charisma she lacked. After shaking hands with Dregs, she sat down next to Free.

"He strove for the good life and made it big. Please welcome our success story of the year, Mr. Harrison Foxtrot!"

Delirious screams of rapturous ecstasy cascaded from the younger females in the audience as Harrison came out in an impeccably tailored business suit and sunglasses. Obviously enjoying the adulation, he removed his sunglasses and picked out several of the more desirable looking young females for personal eye contact and gestures of affection. He tossed business cards in their direction. When his applause began to die down, he took his seat.

"And finally, I bring to you a woman who sees beyond our physical world into the mysteries of the cosmic. An entity of powerful insight, please welcome Ms. Misty Greentree!"

The orchestra reverted to strange, clanging new age music as Misty entered with her hands together, as if in a daze. She gave a somewhat mechanical acknowledgement to the audience and sat down. Almost immediately, her trancelike aura was broken when she saw that she was seated next to her former husband. Instantly, she sprang to her feet and tapped Scott Free on the shoulder, insisting that they trade places. Much too slowly for Misty's taste, he rose and complied with her wish.

"Okay, is everyone happy now?" said Dregs, clearly irritated by the interruption. "Can we continue with the show?"

When all nodded approval he strode to the opposite side of the stage before calling out again to the audience. "And now—a woman who has been a blight to our society—a woman who spreads hate and calls it love—a woman who disdains science in favor of proclaiming a non-existent, brutal deity, please show your disgust for our fraud of the day—a so called born again Christian!"

The orchestra remained silent. A young woman emerged

to a torrent of boos, hisses, and profane epithets. So alone she looked, yet so dignified amidst the sea of hostility. An uncontrollable impulse surged into Seeker. She ran from the back of the audience and up on to the stage.

"Runaway! What are you doing here? I didn't think I'd ever see you again."

"I didn't think you'd see me again either," she calmly replied. "But I have been reborn."

As if on cue, the panel and audience erupted in derisive laughter. Dregs motioned for Seeker to remain on the far side of the stage and brought Runaway to the center.

"So," he said. "You say you're a born again, whatever that is. But we know what you are. And we're going to prove today that you're no better than any of the rest of us. In fact, you are far worse. Let's start off with your ridiculous claim to a monopoly on the truth. How can you possibly make such a narrow-minded assertion, when everyone knows that there are many truths?"

"First of all," responded Runaway in a clear, confident tone. "It is not my truth. There is a God in heaven above who hates sin and loves righteousness. He is the source of all truth. He is..."

"Hold on! Stop right there," interrupted Dregs. "What do you think about her statement, panel?"

"Why does she refer to the Creator as a he?" questioned Misty.

"Sin? Righteousness? Truth? Ain't got no clue what the faith chick be talkin' about," said Frcc.

"I never got any heavenly help. My success came entirely on my own," added Harrison.

"Next thing you know, she'll be spouting off those offensive, outdated Ten Commandments," came the scornful voice of Doctor Fallacious.

Misty Greentree sprang to her feet, waving a scroll like a conductor's baton before the audience. "I have come up with a new, more progressive Ten Pillars of Enlightenment!" she proudly declared.

"Bravo Ms. Greentree! Why don't you read them to us?" said Dregs.

"I will," she dreamily answered. "I'm very happy.

1. You are the final arbiter of your own personal truth.
2. All matter is the god force and is to be worshipped accordingly.
3. Faith in a personal, creator God is vain.
4. Remember Earth Day, and revere it always.

5. Question parental authority. They have no right to impose their beliefs on you.
6. Survival of the fittest is the universal law of nature.
7. All forms of sexual expression are created equal.
8. You are entitled to whatever you need from those who have too much.
9. The greatest gain falls to the cleverest of speech.
10. Self-Realization above all. Pleasure is your greatest end."

As she triumphantly sat down, the audience erupted in cheers, whistles, and thunderous applause. "Bravo again!" cried Dregs above the din. "We have taken another progressive step in our upward evolutionary development!"

He turned disdainfully to Runaway. "I suppose you don't think much of our Ten Pillars of Enlightenment?"

"God's laws are not subject to the whims of men," she answered quietly.

"Who cares what men think?" sneered Doctor Fallacious. "Those words were written by a woman. And you have no right to come here to peddle your patriarchal puritanical propaganda!"

"I thought I was invited here to express my beliefs."

"Well—that's a wrap for today," exalted Dregs. "I think

we have proven beyond a doubt the menace this dangerous woman and her spurious beliefs pose to our society. Thank you all for watching the Dregs Donotrooth Show, those of you here in our studio audience, and those of you watching nationwide on television. In closing, always remember—life is short. Pet a dog and trade in your SUV."

What that the dancers returned to the stage as the orchestra played a rousing, closing tune. Dregs began to shake hands with the panel guests. Runaway was left to herself, ignored on the stage.

Suddenly, the party atmosphere was interrupted by the angry shouts of a woman from the rear of the auditorium. "Hold on! Now you wait just a minute!"

A shabbily dressed, stooped woman made her way to the front and laboriously climbed the steps at the side of the stage. She took a moment to catch her breath before again speaking.

"This is an outrage! You bring this poor young girl here with your hypocritical pretensions of kindness. Then you hit her from all sides and give her no chance to respond. The only fraud you've exposed today is your own smug intolerance! Now you give this girl a chance to speak!"

Momentarily taken aback, Dregs quickly recovered his composure. The hint of a devious smile formed on his face.

"Very well, Baglad*y*. We're always fair around here."

He turned to Runaway. "Go for it, Runaway. Humor us with some of your notions of morality."

Runaway gestured grateful acknowledgment to Baglady and asked that she be provided a chair. Once it was afforded, she came again to the center of the stage and faced out to the audience, which had grown strangely quiet.

"I didn't come here to tell you all how you have to live your lives. All I know is that my life was out of control. I was so lost in guilt and despair, that I no longer wanted to live.

"But one day a woman named Grace, who worked at the local rescue mission, found me curled up on a park bench. She spoke kind words to me and invited me to the mission for a meal and a shower. She gave me clean clothes. It was the first time since I ran away from my home that anyone was kind to me without wanting something in return—except for my two friends seated there at the side. Grace listened to me while I poured out my aching heart and wept bitter tears over the things I had done. And then she told me how all my sins could be forgiven through the cross of Jesus Christ. It was like a light came on in my soul. And there was born in me that day something I had long since discarded—hope. I believed in Jesus Christ. And as the shower made me clean on the outside, so He washed me clean on the inside."

From the depths of her soul poured forth a song.

I started out on a path of life that swept me away
I thought that I had the strength to
stand and hold my ground
But I slipped and found
When I was weak You were strong
You grabbed my hand I'm holding on
And looking in Your eyes I see that I am...

Beautiful, I've been made beautiful
I've been set free,
I've been made whole,
I've been reborn
Beautiful, I've been made beautiful
And by his grace I'll make it through,
For I have been made new

I know that my heart has been tainted
by the things I have done
For so long I have tried to conceal all these scars

And I've tried so hard
But You touch my heart and heal my pain
And fill my soul with love again

I am beautiful, I've been made beautiful
I've been set free,
I've been made whole,
I've been reborn
Beautiful, I've been made beautiful
And by his grace I'll make it through,
For I have been made new

And no matter how I stray in this life
You're always waiting for me to come home
And no matter how I fall You are there
Holding Your hand out
Picking me up You call me
Beautiful, I've been made beautiful

Runaway peered out over the massed throng, many of whom now openly wept, as did she herself. "And I am eternally grateful to Him for taking away my sins and making me a new person. I have done some terrible things in my life. But all are nailed to the cross and buried with Christ in the tomb. And as He rose from the dead, so too my life has now been raised again with Him!"

As Runaway fell silent, Baglady quietly stood to her feet and joined her at the center of the stage. "Is there any hope for someone like me?"

"There is hope, not only for you, but for everyone in this room."

With those words, the quiet of the moment was suddenly broken as Doctor Olga Fallacious erupted in fury. "Ha! I have never heard more presumptive, hate-filled vitriol in all my life! I was born okay the first time—and you have no right to force your beliefs on the rest of us!"

"I got just one problem with the faith chick," added Scott Free. "All that stuff she says gets in my way. Scott Free always does what he wants."

Free rose from his chair, took another healthy gulp from his jug, and headed for the stage right exit. On his way, he began to stagger. His jug dropped to the floor, just before he himself fell with a thud that resounded throughout the auditorium.

Doctor Fallacious strode over to him and gave a cursory examination, confirming what she already knew.

"The fool! I told him to drink only from sterilized containers!"

She picked up his jug and confronted Runaway, holding the container up in her face. "This is completely your fault! You forced the end of the safe poison drinking program in our city." She flung the container on the floor. "And now many more will die because of your narrow dogma and hateful rhetoric. You are a murderer and this is war! And you have no idea what you're up against!"

Runaway declined to respond as Doctor Fallacious stormed from the stage. Upon her exit, Misty approached the young woman to say her piece.

"I am happy that you have found a way to salvation. All channels are true to those who seek. May your path take you to future discoveries of further enlightenment." With that she floated more than walked to the exit.

Finally, Harrison, a great deal more slowly, addressed Runaway, his head bowed low in sorrow and shame. "I may look successful on the outside. The truth is—I'm a mess."

"I can't say that I agree with you," said Dregs. "But I do admire your sincerity. And I must admit that whatever else you might be, you are not a fraud."

"I am a forgiven fraud," responded Runaway.

Dregs humbly nodded and left. Runaway turned her attention to Harrison and Baglady.

"Do you both want to give your lives to Jesus Christ?"

"Yes," Harrison simply replied.

Baglady nodded affirmatively, tears streaming down her cheeks. Runaway offered her hand to Baglady, as Baglady had once offered her hand to Runaway. She took it. The three moved to the side of the stage, where Seeker remained.

The words "If anyone wishes to come after Me, let him deny himself, and take up his cross daily, and follow Me," flashed in Seeker's mind.

"Not yet," she responded to the unasked question.

Without a word, Runaway led the other two from the stage to join some one hundred and fifty people from the audience who had assembled at the front, also wanting to hear the words of eternal life. There they were joined by Grace and the man in the funny looking suit, who stood with them. Among those who came forward, noted Seeker, was another familiar face—Gullible.

She observed those who were leaving, most of whom were doing so respectfully. A few lingered and watched from a distance. *They probably hesitate for the same reason as I*, she thought. A few others looked like they wanted to make trouble, but some sort of field seemed to surround those who had gathered at the front that kept them from their purpose.

The scene faded from view and I last saw Seeker back in the Lifestyle Shoppe. Though this time she did not need the towel, she appeared more miserable than ever.

"Well Seeker," inquired the shopkeeper. "Have you decided where you are going to buy?"

"Not yet," she answered. "But at least I know why I cannot. It is simply a matter of the will."

The shopkeeper nodded. "It is good that you can at least be honest with yourself. And I am content to be patient. Sooner or later, everyone buys from the Lifestyle Shoppe."

Printed in the United States
By Bookmasters